For Jane Gardam the best sound in the world is "a child laughing out loud at a book", and her books have been making children laugh and think for many years. Among them are the Walker Double *Black Woolly Pony, White Chalk Horse* and the Walker Story Book *The Kit Stories*. Her books for older readers include *A Few Fair Days* and *The Hollow Land*, which won the Whitbread Children's Novel Award. She has also won major prizes for her adult books. Jane Gardam is married with three grown-up children and lives in an old house in Kent, which has the ruins of a monastery and a chapel in the garden – and, some say, even a ghost!

Peter Melnyczuk is a freelance illustrator. His books for children include *While Shepherds Watched*, the Read and Wonder title *Red Fox* (by Karen Wallace) and *The Giant's Boot* (by Charles Ashton), which was shortlisted for the Smarties Book Prize.

*Harry went down the lane to the beach looking
back all the time at Tufty Bear.*

TUFTY BEAR

Written by
JANE GARDAM

Illustrated by
PETER MELNYCZUK

WALKER BOOKS
AND SUBSIDIARIES
LONDON • BOSTON • SYDNEY

For Imogen and Julie

First published 1996 by Walker Books Ltd
87 Vauxhall Walk, London SE11 5HJ

This edition published 1997

2 4 6 8 10 9 7 5 3

Text © 1996 Jane Gardam
Illustrations © 1996 Peter Melnyczuk

This book has been typeset in Plantin.

Printed in England by Clays Ltd, St Ives plc

British Library Cataloguing in Publication Data
A catalogue record for this book is
available from the British Library.

ISBN 0-7445-4750-4

J 110, 244
£3.99

CONTENTS

*Harry looked out of the window and saw a bear
sitting on the gatepost.*

TUFTY BEAR

Harry looked out of the window and saw a bear sitting on the gatepost.

It was very early in the morning and not quite light. He ran to the next bedroom where his mother and father were deep asleep with their feet sticking out here and there from the end of the bed.

"There's a bear sitting on the gatepost."

Grumble, grunt.

"It has its arms stretched out."

"Go back to bed, Harry." Grumble, grunt. "It was a dream."

Harry tickled the soles of some feet.

"Yow! Hey! Harry! Go back to bed. It's the

middle of the night. It was a dream."

"A dream..." said his mother dreamily, pulling in her feet. "Bed..."

Harry went back to his room. He pulled back the pink curtains again and looked out of the window. The bear was gone.

It was the very beginning of the holiday. As they were setting off for the beach after breakfast, a red post-van was going by. It stopped and the postman got out. "Morning," he said. "Find your bear then?"

"Bear?" said Mum.

"Lying by the gate. Just out in the lane. I put him up on the gatepost yesterday morning. Thought you must have dropped him."

"We weren't here yesterday morning," said Harry's father. "We didn't arrive until after dark. We didn't see any bears."

"He was there before breakfast," said Harry. "I told you. You've forgotten."

"He's still here now," said the postman. "See those feet?" and he lifted from the middle of a bramble bush, where he had been balancing on his nose, a particularly friendly-looking tufty bear. He still had his arms stretched out and he still seemed to be looking at Harry.

"Can he come with us? Oh, can he come with us to the beach? He's *asking* to come," said Harry.

The postman and Harry's parents looked thoughtful.

"There's probably someone looking everywhere for him," said Harry's mum. "I think we should leave him on the gatepost for one more day."

"Not all day," said Harry. "*Please* not all day."

"Seems a bit hard," said the postman. "They had their chance yesterday, who ever they were who let him get lost."

"And anyone might pick him up," said Harry's father, "whether he's theirs or not. He's a lovely bear. We're being very trusting, just leaving him here for anybody."

"Sometimes you *should* be trusting," said Harry's mother.

In the end they left him, with a note pinned on the gate saying, "Is this your bear?"

People came up and down the sandy lane all day, back and forth to the sea, with picnics and bags and baskets and folding chairs and toys and buckets and beach-towels and model aeroplanes and blow-up air beds and boats and ice-creams and babies who cried and babies who didn't cry and babies lying zonked out flat in their buggies. Perhaps everyone had their hands so full that they didn't have time to read the notice, for when Harry and his parents came trudging up the lane at the end of the day by the sea, all tousled up and comfortable and their shoes so full of sand it hardly seemed worth having dragged them stickily on to their feet – when they reached their gate again, the bear was still sitting there with his arms stretched out towards Harry.

"He's there!" Harry shouted, suddenly running. "He's ours."

"He really is a very, very nice bear," said his father. "An old-fashioned bear. I think we ought to leave him one more day. He's not just anyone. He must have a history."

"We can't leave him out all night," said Mum. "It might rain. We'll put him back on the gatepost in the morning."

Harry's father lifted the bear down and Harry took it in his arms, chest to chest. During supper the bear sat on the kitchen table, watching Harry with his bright black glass eyes.

He was no ordinary bear. He was black and white but not like a panda, for his fur was tufty and white and he had big black stitches for claws and a round black nose and a very kind black mouth. He was solid and warm-looking as if there were a beating heart inside him.

"He's called Tufty Bear," said Harry.

Tufty Bear looked quite agreeable about this.

"Come on, Tufty Bear, to bed," said Harry's mother.

Tufty Bear watched Harry in the bath.

"He looks quite a talkative sort," said Harry's mother.

Tufty Bear watched Harry in the bath.

"He's saying 'Where's your fur?'," said Harry.

Tufty Bear went on watching Harry from the end of the bed as Harry got in under the squashy duvet and curled round.

"This is *my* fur," said Harry.

"Very strange," said Tufty Bear. "I don't take mine on and off like that. Mind, I do feel cold sometimes. Like now. It's better than last night on that gatepost with spiders running all over me and frightening noises in the hedge, and the wind toppling me in the brambles. But I *am* rather cold."

"And my nose is still sore," he said, after a minute.

"You'd better come in under my fur," said Harry. So Tufty Bear spent a very comfortable night with his head beside Harry's, smiling up at the ceiling.

* * *

14

"He should have been washed first," said Harry's mum. "We don't know where he's been."

"He looks very clean," said Harry's father. "He's very particularly clean. He looks as if he's just out of his packing. Yet he's an old bear. You don't see these lovely ones about any more. They're all nylon now. This one is cotton and wool and all the stitches are made by hand."

"Can he come to the beach with us? Please, please, *please*," yearned Harry.

They looked uncertain.

"I think we ought to put him on the gatepost again. Just one more day," said Mum.

That morning Harry went down the lane to the beach, looking back over his shoulder all the time at Tufty Bear seated on the gatepost holding out his beseeching arms. It was getting windy and the day was damp but there were still lots of people passing to and fro, in the lane. Harry saw some of them stop and read the notice. He heard his father say, "You were wrong, Kim. People will nick anything these days. They'll just take him. Who's to know whether he belongs to them or not. We've seen the last of that bear."

His father took the trouble to play with Harry all that day. He built a sand-castle. He dug a canal going down to the sea. He lifted Harry over the seaweed that wraps up your legs in slithery ribbons, over the rattling hungry pebbles at the sea's edge and into the clear water. He began to teach Harry to swim.

They watched the water-skiers and the sand-yachts. They bought ice-creams with smooth squirls on the top.

At lunch time Mum said she had forgotten

the apples and went back to the cottage. Harry heard her whisper when she came back, "He's still there."

At the end of the day Harry went tearing ahead of his parents up the sandy lane, weaving in and out of the other people going home from the sea, some of them cross, some of them hungry, some of them tired, all of them wind-swept, with sand tickling in their hair and between their toes.

In and out he ran until he saw Sandy Cottage and a little group standing outside the gate looking at Tufty Bear.

Tufty Bear seemed to have a non-smile on his face now and his arms were not very welcoming. The group dwindled away.

"Where is the notice?" said Dad.

The notice seemed to have disappeared.

"Did you pull it down?" asked Harry at supper time, but Tufty Bear didn't seem talkative tonight. He merely stared.

In bed later, though, Harry thought he heard him say, "*Very* difficult getting out the drawing pins. *Very* hard indeed. I hope that's the end of it I'm sure."

The next day they didn't put Tufty Bear on the gatepost. They put up a notice by itself saying:

FOUND
Very nice teddy
bear. Apply
within.

and they left it on the gate for the rest of the holiday.

But nobody came, and when it was time to go home Tufty Bear went with them. He rode in the back of the car with Harry, looking settled and seeming very pleased with the scenery.

He seemed a bit less pleased when they reached the motorway – as if he wished he could close his glass eyes against all the whizzing and the flashing lights. And when they came to the miles of streets of the city, he looked amazed. Aeroplanes zipped overhead. Police sirens wailed.

"I don't know how you stand it," he said to Harry after supper, nose tipped forward against the window pane watching the traffic passing in the street below like streams of coloured beetles.

"Can't you get them to go and live by the sea all the time?"

"No," said Harry, "Dad has to work here."

"What is work?" asked Tufty Bear.

"You don't know anything, do you?" said Harry.

"I know I like you," said Tufty Bear. "I don't care where I live as long as I can stay with you lot."

"You're a good friend," said Harry.

The very next day Harry went with his mother to the supermarket to stock up with food again after the holiday.

He was really too old to sit in the basket of the shopping trolley. His legs trailed down. But he wanted Tufty Bear to see properly even though it was a squash.

Mum shoved and heaved and in the end said, "It's too heavy, Harry, with so much shopping," and she hauled him out of the basket, getting his feet a bit tangled on the way.

Tufty Bear fell from under his arm into the

trolley of the person behind him.

A girl a bit younger than Harry screeched out, "Mum! Look! It's our bear!"

Before she'd finished saying it Harry had grabbed Tufty Bear and barricaded himself behind the trolley, with Tufty Bear held behind his back.

"It's *my* bear! It's *my* bear!" roared the girl.

"It's *my* bear! It's *my* bear!" roared Harry.

"I hate you," shrieked the girl.

"I hate you back," yelled Harry.

The girl's mother said, "*Tilly*! What is all this about? Be quiet this minute. Now! Don't be so silly."

"Harry," cried his mum, "how dare you —"

"I'm so sorry," said the girl's mother. "We lost a bear on holiday and she's been in a terrible state. She thinks every bear she sees... She's been like this for over a week.

21

We had to leave our holiday cottage without it."

"Where were you on holiday?" asked Harry's mum in a very flat voice, and Harry brought Tufty Bear from behind his back and zipped him up inside his jacket where he didn't at all fit.

"Sandy Cottage, Sandy Lane, Windy Ridge, Dorset," said the girl's mum.

"So were we," said Harry's mum.

The two mothers looked at each other.

"We saw the advert for it in the corner shop."

"So did we. We live in London Place."

"We live just round the corner."

Tilly began to howl and scream again and launched herself on Harry. Harry became all arms and legs and blazing eyes and began to biff Tilly with Tufty Bear pulled out of his jacket.

*Harry became all arms and legs and blazing eyes and
began to biff Tilly with Tufty Bear.*

"We'd better go to the coffee shop and sort this out," said Harry's mum, and the four of them sat there, Harry now keeping Tufty Bear well out of sight below the table edge, firmly fixed behind his knees.

"Actually," said Tilly's mum, "I'd better tell you the whole story. That bear was never really ours at all. We found it in Sandy Cottage, lying on the bed Tilly had, in the room with the pink curtains. She lost it in the garden. She'd been playing near the gate. We looked everywhere. We decided it must have been stolen by someone going down the lane. It was awful. He was a special sort of bear. We didn't know what to do. I wrote to the owners in the end to tell them, but they haven't replied. They're still away on their own holidays. I'm dreading them coming back. I suppose it *is* the same bear?"

"Could we look at Tufty Bear please

Harry?" asked his mum, and very, very slowly Harry removed Tufty Bear from between the chair and the back of his knees and sat him on the table, holding him tightly with both hands.

As soon as she saw Tufty Bear Tilly began to howl.

"Yes, it is. No doubt about it I'm afraid," said her mum.

"We found him – well the postman found him in the brambles near the gate," said Harry's mum.

"I *won't* give him up," said Harry.

"I want my beeeeaar," wailed Tilly.

"What is the next step?" asked Tilly's mum.

The two mothers took each others' telephone numbers and decided to go home and think about things. Harry's mum asked Tilly's mum if they could come to tea tomorrow and, "Harry," she said, "I would be very proud of you now if you would let Tilly have Tufty Bear just for tonight."

But Harry's face turned into a thunder storm.

"No. Don't upset him," said Tilly's mum and she gathered Tilly up and left with Tilly's feet kicking behind her like somebody trying to swim from a shipwreck and her face in front roaring like a sea-monster.

"Dreadful," everybody said in the coffee shop.

"Nobody brings children up properly now."

This made both mothers even crosser.

"I'm *afraid*," said Harry's dad that night, "that Tufty Bear will have to go back again to Sandy Cottage, Harry. It's his home. He has an owner already. He is not ours and he's not Tilly's. We shall all have to go back next year to see him."

"He *can't*," said Harry. "He'll die of loneliness. I'll die of loneliness. I'll run away. I'll go and live there with him. I hate everybody."

"I am ashamed of you, Harry," said both his parents.

In Tilly's house Tilly's mother was saying, "I am ashamed of you, Tilly. It's only a bear. That little boy thought it was going to be his for ever. *We* knew it really belonged to Sandy Cottage. You couldn't have brought it home anyway."

"Next year we'll go to Spain," said Tilly's father, and that set Tilly off again.

That night Harry woke and saw that Tufty Bear was watching him. They were nose to nose in the moonlight.

"What's the matter, Tufty Bear?" he asked.

"I keep thinking of Tilly," said Tufty Bear. "A nice girl. I'd forgotten her. She was silly to lose me but she seems to be fond of me."

"You don't mean you want to go and live with her instead?"

"No-o," said Tufty Bear. "Actually, though, I do keep thinking of Sandy Cottage. It's nice there. I was used to it. Plenty of time to think. You could hear the swish of the sea. People didn't get into states and squeeze you about and throw you around and use you as a hammer."

"Sorry," said Harry.

"And, you know, you don't have to be with even *best* friends all the time. As long as you know you'll see them again and that they like you. It makes something to look forward to."

"You'd have to be posted," said Harry.

"That might be quite fun," said Tufty Bear. "By the way. I saw your father come in and put something under your pillow while you were asleep just now."

But Harry had fallen asleep again.

In the morning two things happened.

Under Harry's pillow was a present called *A Book of Bears* so glorious, with such wonderful bear photographs taken in such exciting countries far away, that Tufty Bear got left under the bedclothes while Harry had breakfast.

Secondly, there came a knock on Harry's front door and it was Tilly and Tilly's mum, all smiles and not waiting till teatime.

Tilly's mum flapped a letter in her hand. It was from the owner of Sandy Cottage who had come home. It said:

> Please do not worry. I am
> sure our bear will turn up.
> We shall find him again and put
> him back in the room with the
> pink curtains for next time you
> come here.
> That bear never strays far.

"Now I can write and explain," said Harry's mum. "Where is Tufty Bear at present, Harry?"

"Oh, somewhere about," said Harry, reading his book.

Tilly was busy with Harry's train set.

Then the owner of Tufty Bear wrote to Harry's mother and said:

> There's no hurry to return
> the bear. Harry and Tilly can
> share him until you all come
> back next year. I'm glad he's
> brought you all together.

"Can Tilly take him to her house next week and you have him the week after and go on like that?" asked Harry's mum. "Share him?"

"I'll come and see him over here," said Tilly, busy with an engine.

"Or we could just post him back," said Harry, and everyone looked surprised. "He might be ready for his own home again."

"What do you think, Tilly?" asked her mum.

"All right," said Tilly.

And so they did.

Next year the two families went to Sandy Cottage, Sandy Lane, Windy Ridge, Dorset together. Tufty Bear was waiting for them with his arms stretched out to everyone.

*Then somebody stepped out of Tilly's car
carrying a big knitted bag.*

Tufty Bear and the Knitting Granny

Tufty Bear was in a bedroom window of Sandy Cottage with his nose pressed against the glass so that he would see Harry and Tilly the moment they arrived.

Harry's car came first and out stepped Harry and his mum and dad.

Then somebody stepped out of Tilly's car carrying a big knitted bag. She was wearing a knitted dress and a knitted hat and even what looked like knitted shoes. Out of the knitted bag stuck lots of knitting needles and great bundles of very bright knitting wool.

Blinking hard, Tufty Bear saw that Tilly, Tilly's mum and Tilly's dad were all wearing enormous buttercup-coloured knitted sweaters down to their knees, and they were looking rather glum.

The lady was taken over to meet Harry and his mum and dad. Up and down went her handshake, up and down went her head and smile, smile went her mouth. Suddenly she pounced down into her knitted bag and took out a tape and began to measure Harry all over. Harry squirmed and wriggled and then – horrible! – he gave the lady a push.

Trouble here, thought Tufty Bear.

Feet on the stairs and in flew Harry and Tilly to Tufty Bear's bedroom and Tufty Bear was plucked from the window. Then he was hugged and then he was tossed into the air, and then he was cheered, hurrah.

"The summer's begun," said Tufty Bear.

"Roll on winter."

"Don't be such a misery, Tufty Bear," said Harry. "You know we love you. We haven't seen you since Easter. Twelve weeks."

"Twelve weeks of peace," said Tufty Bear. "Twelve weeks in the quiet of a still, dark cupboard. Time for thoughts. I don't know why I am so fond of you. Who is the lady made of knitting?"

"She's my granny," said Tilly. "She knits like crazy. You can't stop her."

"I saw Harry being very horrible to her," said Tufty Bear. "Not the way to treat an old lady."

"She was going to cover me in knitting," said Harry.

"Look what she's done to all of us," said Tilly. "My dad says we look like three plates of scrambled eggs."

"And very delicious," said Tufty Bear.

"There's many a bear would like to have someone care for him so kindly."

"She seems to talk a lot, your Knitting Granny," said Harry. "Will she be staying all the holiday?"

"One week," said Tilly. "And she's going to baby-sit in the evening too. So we'll have to put up with her."

"That is not the way to speak of a granny," said Tufty Bear, "and as for talking a lot – what about you two? You don't need any lessons in that. Ha! She approaches."

The Knitting Granny's feet were on the verandah of Sandy Cottage. The Knitting Granny's voice went chatter, chatter in the passage of Sandy Cottage.

The Knitting Granny could be heard filling a kettle for tea in the kitchen and saying that a tea-cosy would be nice for this teapot and she had some lovely purple wool just right, and she could make egg-cosies to match.

Then up the stairs came the Knitting Granny, calling for Harry and Tilly to come to tea – and she saw Tufty Bear. And suddenly Tufty Bear looked very much as if he hadn't any clothes.

Tilly took him and hid him under a pillow.

"*Well* now, Tilly, what a funny thing to do. Hiding Teddy. I suppose you're not meant to have him."

"Yes we are," said Tilly and Harry together.

"He belongs to Sandy Cottage," said Harry, "but they leave him out for us."

"Actually he did live with *us* once," said Tilly.

"Now, now. Don't tell naughty lies," said the Knitting Granny.

"Ask mum then," said Harry. "He is one of the reasons for coming to Sandy Cottage.

We took him home last time by mistake and we had to post him back. They said they'd leave him for us this time in the window."

"What kind people." The Knitting Granny fished him out from under the pillow. She twirled his head about and tapped it to see if it rocked and then left it looking out over the back of his neck.

"Quite an old teddy. I could stitch his head on tighter. Oh dear, his claws are getting un-ravelled. I'll pick them out and re-sew them. I have a very nice *orange* wool. I will make him a new *orange* nose to match, and maybe some *orange* soles to his feet."

"Never!" shouted Harry.

"NO!" shrieked Tilly.

And with Tufty Bear's head under Tilly's arm, they ran with him into the garden and hid him in some sandy bushes.

* * *

At supper the Knitting Granny wasn't a bit upset. The parents had gone for a walk so the Knitting Granny, full speed ahead, had Harry and Tilly bathed and in their night clothes and eating supper; then upstairs, prayers, teeth and into bed.

"Is it a race?" asked Harry. "It's only afternoon."

"All little boys and girls should be in bed by six o'clock," said the Knitting Granny, "and I have something special to do. Now, where's that funny old teddy?"

"He's *not* 'Teddy'," said Harry. "He's Tufty Bear."

"He's not here," said Tilly. (*And you won't find him*, she thought.)

"I expect he's in the garden," said the Knitting Granny. "Off to sleep," and she went into the garden and started rooting about.

"Whatever shall we do if she changes him?" Harry asked Tilly.

Tilly began to cry and so that he wouldn't start too, Harry began to make jet-plane noises and crash the bed about. Their parents, coming home, heard the racket and hurried upstairs to say goodnight.

"Now don't worry," they said, "we wouldn't let anyone change Tufty Bear."

"Do you want him up here?" asked Harry's dad. "It is his bedroom after all."

"Yes *now*," said Harry. "It's so *early*. We'll be awake for hours."

But when Harry's father came back with Tufty Bear, both Harry and Tilly were asleep. So Tufty Bear's head was turned the right way round and he was laid carefully on the window sill where all night long he stared thoughtfully at the moon.

* * *

Next morning on the beach everything was lovely. The sun shone hotly and the cheerful waves came splashing in. There were wonderful squiggly things in the rock pools, games to play and somebody flew a kite that plunged about like mad snakes. Everybody was slapped about with sun-block cream and the ice-creams in the kiosk were messy and gorgeous.

Tufty Bear had been left at home to be out of dangers. "He is a bear with an adventurous streak," said Harry's father.

"I have *plans* for what will happen to that teddy," said the Knitting Granny, who was sitting a little way off on a knitted blanket. She was knitting fast, something white and small.

Harry and Tilly were filling buckets for a moat or they would have shivered.

* * *

That night it was baked beans and bananas and bed and sleep as fast as the night before, and nobody complaining. Harry and Tilly even forgot to say goodnight to Tufty Bear. They didn't even see that he was gone from the window ledge. They were zonked.

But at breakfast next day – oh help! In the middle of the table, between the marmalade and the seven purple eggcups, sat Tufty Bear in frilly knitted pants!

Harry and Tilly could not meet his eyes.

And the Knitting Granny sat on the beach with a smile on her face all day long except for when she was dishing out lovely sandwiches and home-made lemonade (she was wonderful at picnics) and talking all the time about surprises.

"There will be a surprise every day of the week," she said. And oh, my word, there was!

*In the middle of the table sat Tufty Bear in
frilly knitted pants!*

The frilly pants were on the Sunday.

On Monday came a lacy vest.

On Tuesday came some dainty knitted shoes.

On Wednesday came a little fairy-bag with a *hanky* sticking out.

On Thursday was a sun bonnet.

On Friday there was nothing.

But …

On Saturday came a frilly dress with rows of ruffles and puff sleeves, sugar pink and frothy as foam.

It had taken two full days and inside it was Tufty Bear's stout body and above it glared his fine black-nosed face.

And the face was saying:

I am a bear.

I am not Miss Muffet.

I am not the fairy on the Christmas tree.

I am Tufty Bear.

"Well," said Harry's mum nervously, "you *are* kind. You *have* worked hard. Harry, say 'thank you' to Tilly's Granny."

"Yes. Say 'thank you', Tilly," said Tilly's mum, weakly.

Harry's dad rattled the newspaper.

Tilly's dad went off to get the beach things together for Granny's last day. Harry and Tilly didn't say anything.

It began to rain a bit and Harry and Tilly had to play on the verandah until it stopped. They could not look at Tufty Bear, it was too shaming. He stayed rigid on the table.

But when the sun came out and everything steamed, Harry dropped him into a beach bag.

While everyone was unpacking the rugs and chairs on the sand, Harry fished him out again and with Tilly went off among the rocks and took off all Tufty Bear's clothes and put them out of sight.

At long, long last Tufty Bear gave a great sigh. "Good afternoon," he said. "I am very much obliged. What do you propose to do with them?"

"We don't know. Something or other," said Tilly.

"We'll have to put them on you again before we go home," said Harry. "She'll be very hurt if we don't."

"I am the one who's been hurt," said Tufty Bear. "I am sitting here wondering what my life has become. After all my noble years, to be kitted out in *sun bonnets*. You never know what is round the corner in this world."

There was a dazzle of lightning, a huge clap of thunder and rain began to fall on the beach as if someone was emptying a gigantic bucket.

"You see what I mean," said Tufty Bear.

Everyone ran for the lane and Sandy Cottage, Tufty Bear safe under Harry's tee-shirt.

In bed that night Tilly said, "Harry, we left the clothes behind."

Harry was very quiet. "They'll be washed away by now," he said.

They looked at Tufty Bear, who was in with Tilly tonight.

"Hurrah," said Harry, but with a sort of question mark.

"Good," said Tilly, uncertainly.

Tufty Bear said, "She was very kind, you know. I hope she won't think we did it on purpose."

"She's leaving today," said Harry, very thoughtfully.

At breakfast, there sat the Knitting Granny

all ready to be taken to the train in her knitted hat and coat and her knitted bag full of her tickets and snapshots of the holiday and her knitted purse. Out of her knitted purse she took two pound coins, one each for Harry and Tilly.

"You have been very good," she said. "I shall miss you. And I shall miss Teddy. Now, Harry and Tilly, I have something very sad to tell you. Somehow we left all Teddy's new clothes on the beach. I went to find them last night and put them on the stove to dry and they have all shrunk. They will never fit poor Teddy again. So if you don't mind, I'm taking them home for a small doll I know."

"That's all right," said Harry.

"Tufty Bear won't mind," said Tilly.

"As a matter of fact," said the Knitting Granny, "I wasn't sure about those clothes anyway. I rather like a teddy to look like a bear."

Tufty Bear, in his own tufty fur, lying among the purple eggcups on the table, looked high up out of the kitchen window.

"I'll never understand human beings," he said to Harry. "Never. Maybe it's the heat. Roll on Christmas."

There stood Sandy Cottage in a cloud of whirling snow-flakes.

TUFTY BEAR AND THE
FIGHTING GRANDAD

Everybody so loved Sandy Cottage that they all decided to go there together for Christmas – Harry, Tilly, two dads and two mums.

They took all the presents with them, the Christmas tree, the tinsel, the mistletoe and holly.

They took the Christmas pudding and the turkey and the chestnuts and the big iced Christmas cake and a huge pink ham.

They took paper and string and parcel tags and all the Christmas cards.

They took warm clothes and books to read and tapes to play.

They took firelighters and matches and even logs of wood, and wellies and water-proofs.

Both mums took their recipe books.

The day they all set off it was beginning to snow and the town was being thinly painted white.

"Sandy Cottage won't be in the snow," said Tilly's father, "it doesn't often snow by the sea. The sea keeps the land warm."

Tilly and Harry were cross. It was miserable to leave a white Christmas behind them.

But as they drew near, the snow became thicker and thicker, and there stood Sandy Cottage on a white carpet in a cloud of whirling snow-flakes. Even its windows were almost covered up and Tufty Bear, whose place was on the window sill of the room with pink curtains, was nowhere to be seen.

But inside, there he was on Harry's bed with
a note pinned on him by his owners saying:

Window sill
too cold
for bears
at Christmas

"Too cold for you lot, too, I should have
thought," said Tufty Bear. "Fancy leaving all
the fun of the town for a summer cottage full
of cracks to let the cold in. I had had half a
hope, I must say, that I'd have been invited
to London instead."

"You hated London, Tufty Bear," said
Tilly. "You know you did. Don't be a
curmudgeon. Here we are."

"Compliments of the freezin' season I'm
sure."

"You are sounding like a peppery old

grandad," said Harry.

"I've not met a grandad," said Tufty Bear. "I've met a granny. I've been thinking about her since the summer."

"My grandad isn't peppery," said Tilly, "he just dodders about."

"My grandad is marvellous," said Harry. "He's great. He's called the Fighting Grandad."

"Is he a boxer?" asked Tilly.

"No, he's just funny. He likes tearing about with a pretend sword and pretend armour and falling down off a pretend horse and lying pretend dead with his legs in the air."

"How very undignified," said Tufty Bear. "Is he very young?"

"No, he's about a hundred," said Harry.

The snow continued to fall. The house was

very cold. The telephone stopped working. The stove was bad-tempered. The gas supply went bubble, bubble, fizzle, phut. There were not enough blankets. Two hot-water bottles leaked.

Outside, Sandy Lane was silent. Nobody went by to the sea. Even the postman didn't call. There were no carol-singers and the church bells from the village sounded far away. Tilly's dad and Harry's dad spread out the tree lights in a network all over the floor and they were as tangled as the Knitting Granny's knitting and half of them didn't work.

Everyone was so cross then that they all muffled up and went for a trudge to the sea, and the sea looked icily at them saying, "Whatever are you doing here *now*?"

The beach looked dark and the sandhills very queer, all powdered with snow. You couldn't believe in kites and sand-castles and ices and sun-burn.

So they all trailed back again to Sandy Cottage, wondering how they would get dry and at last somebody said the awful words that everyone had been trying not to say: *I wish we'd stayed at home.*

But then ... when they opened the cottage door, there seemed to be a difference.

There was a crackling noise from the sitting room where a lovely fire was burning. The curtains had been drawn everywhere and there was a strong smell of hot supper.

In the kitchen, with his feet on the table and his boots beside the stove – a stove that had grown warm and settled and had a big pot bubbling on it – sat an old man with tremendous eyebrows.

It was the Fighting Grandad.

Looking at him across the table was Tufty

Bear and on the floor was a carpet-bag.

"Take cover," roared the Fighting Grandad to Tufty Bear. "Marauders, pirates, press-gangs! Napoleon Bonaparte. Under the table, Bear. Into my travelling bag! Lie Bear-o."

"Grandad!" cried Harry.

"Wherever have you come from?" cried Harry's mum.

"Battlefields of Europe. Oceans of the East. Ice-fields of the North Pole," said the Grandad.

"However did you get here?"

"Magic carpet, catamaran, rubber dinghy, single-screw sea-plane, lift from airport, articulated lorry, motorway, then legs left-right. Very wet. They're on the stove. Boots, not legs. I'm cooking a cannibal stew."

"Or a cannon-ball stew," he said at supper. "Rather chewy. Never mind. I've mended the tree lights. It's Christmas Eve tomorrow. Leave all the work to me."

"However did he manage to bring a cannon-ball stew with him?" asked Tilly in bed that night. "And get all the fires going and make everything warm and funny."

"He just can," said Harry. "He always does. Then he goes away to goodness-knows-where, like a jungle or a desert, and we don't hear from him for ages and ages. He's a wonderful grandad."

"You are lucky, Harry."

"Yes I know. I wish he lived with us always."

"By the way," said Tilly, "where's Tufty Bear?"

"Oh, somewhere about," said Harry. "The Fighting Grandad's taking us out tomorrow on a dog sleigh."

* * *

The dogs were Harry and Tilly joined together with scarves.

The sleigh was the Fighting Grandad being very noisy, running behind and making halloo-ing noises and whirling other scarves in the air for a whip. They hurtled down Sandy Lane and along by the sea that looked cheerier today.

On Christmas Day the sun came out. They walked through the sparkling snow to church, then back again for Christmas dinner. Then there was the tree and the presents and games and the Fighting Grandad did some singing and dancing and sometimes stood on his head.

At bedtime Harry and Tilly fell asleep full of Christmas. The room with the pink curtains had paper and ribbons and new presents and emptied stockings all over the floor. They were very happy, except that there was a small niggle somewhere in Harry's mind. He couldn't think what it was as he went to sleep.

He woke to see Tilly looking out of the window at the early morning and she said, "I think he's going."

"What – my grandad?"

"Yes. He's shovelled a path to the gate and he's standing with his carpet-bag beside him."

Harry sprang out of bed and opened the window and the Fighting Grandad stood to attention in the snow and pretended to blow a trumpet toodle-oooh.

"You *mustn't* go," shouted Tilly.

"Duty calls," cried the Fighting Grandad. "I'm off to Cape Canaveral. I'll send you some rock from the moon."

"He is a crazy man," said Harry's mum at breakfast. "I'm glad he came but he does seem to leave such a mess behind him. You can't get anything done. His room is chaos. He seems to have packed all sorts of things he shouldn't and he's left behind all his dirty socks. By the way, where's Tufty Bear? We haven't seen him all Christmas."

A great dread filled the kitchen.

"Oh no, oh no!" said Harry.

"He *couldn't*," said Tilly.

"D'you know, I believe he has," said Tilly's father. "Didn't he make him hide in his bag? Did he ever get him out again?"

"The old sausage has gone and taken him to the moon," said Harry's father.

"And he *never* sends anything back," said Harry's mother. "He forgets us all the minute after he's gone."

"Oh, whatever shall we do?" wept Tilly.

"What will Tufty Bear's owners say?" wailed Harry.

That night Harry and Tilly lay in their beds in the moonlight that shone bright on the snow, and they were miserable.

"I never even wished him Happy Christmas," said Tilly.

"I haven't had a talk with him for ages," said Harry. "I liked talking to him. He was a grumpy bear but nice and funny."

"He only talked to us," said Tilly. "D'you think he'll talk to your grandad? He might tell him to post him back. He was a very intelligent bear."

"Thanks a bunch," said a voice. "I *don't* think."

"What did you say, Tilly?"

"Nothing," said Tilly. "Someone said 'I *don't* think'."

Behind the pink curtains was a small dark shadow. "I *don't* think," said the shadow. "Nobody could get a word in with that fellow. Never listened. The best place for a *distinguished* bear with the likes of him around is—"

Harry had sprung from his bed and flung back the pink curtains.

"Oh, thank goodness! We thought you'd gone to the moon."

"Or the battlefields of Europe," said Tilly.

"Or the oceans of the East," said Harry.

"Or the ice-fields of the North Pole," said both of them.

"Ridiculous," said Tufty Bear. "Some people can't be happy in their own homes. Very jolly person, but I'm glad he's gone. I'm frozen sitting here. Tuck me in somewhere."

"We'll never forget you again, Tufty Bear," said Tilly.

"We're sorry, Tufty Bear," said Harry bundling him into the blankets. "A Happy New Year."

"People get scatty at Christmas," said Tufty Bear. "Happy New Year to you lot. And roll on the Spring."

THE END